Where on EARTH is the MOON?

by Ruth Martin

illustrated by Olivier Latyk

To Doreen and Steve – O.L.

For Mum, who always watches over me, and for my new baby, Tabitha – R.M.

A TEMPLAR BOOK

This softback edition published in the UK in 2011 by Templar Publishing,
an imprint of The Templar Company Limited,
The Granary, North Street, Dorking, Surrey, RH4 1DN, UK
www.templarco.co.uk

First published in the UK in hardback in 2010 by Templar Publishing

First softback edition

ISBN 978-1-84877-532-9

Designed by Leonard Le Rolland
Edited by Emma Goldhawk

Printed in China

Where on EARTH is the MOON?

by Ruth Martin

illustrated by Olivier Latyk

On the night Luna was born, the full Moon filled up the sky —
brighter than the stars, as round as a button
and bigger than ever before.

As she grew up, Luna watched for the Moon
and saw that it came to check on her at bedtime.

At night, before she climbed into bed, Luna liked to stand
at her bedroom window, with glossy moonlight puddling at her chilly feet.
From there she could see the Moon, sailing on a deep, dark sea of sky.

The Moon was so still and so pretty that Luna always felt soft waves of
sleepiness sloshing over her as she drifted off to sleep.

As she slept, Luna dreamed...

of crescent moons...

of half-moons...

But each morning, when Luna woke up, the Moon had gone.
It was nowhere to be seen in the plain, clear sky.

No stars blinked, no shadows danced across the bedroom floor,
and there were no sparkly moonbeams
to spotlight Luna, standing at the window.

"Where does the Moon go during the day?"
thought Luna.

She pondered...

She puzzled...

She wondered...

and she mooned
about her bedroom
thinking, all day long.

Dusk crept up while Luna thought. Creamy moonbeams spilled in through the window and night-time fell.

Now the Moon was back at last, Luna promised herself she wouldn't let it disappear again.

She would stay awake...

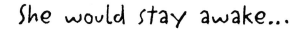

and not go to sleep...

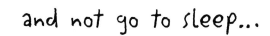

and keep watch for where the Moon might go.

From the window, Luna could see the ocean,
far away in the distance.
As dark as the sky, the water glistened.
Waves whOOshed and washed at the shore.

Luna tried as hard as she could to stay awake.
She wanted to know where the Moon went.
Perhaps it slipped softly into the ocean, she wondered.
WhOOsh wash, whOOsh wash went the waves,
and slowly Luna fell into a dreamy sleep...

Luna's dream took her down into the murky depths of the ocean.

There she found a fish that glowed
and glistened like the Moon...
but no sign of the Moon at all.

The next morning, Luna woke up still wondering
where the Moon might go in the daytime.

She wished the day away and promised
herself she would find out that night.

As night-time came,
Luna looked out at the Moon,
beyond the forest and
over the distant mountains.

ch-ch.. ch-ch chirped the crickets.
Twit-twoo hooted the owls.

Luna tried as hard as she
could to stay awake.

But, before long, she felt herself
falling into a dreamy sleep.

Maybe, she thought,
the Moon rolled
down behind
the mountains,
far, far
away...

Luna's dream took her floating high over the mountains.
There, shimmering and shining, Luna saw a frozen lake
as bright and beautiful as the Moon...

but no sign of the Moon at all.

The next morning, Luna woke up knowing that the Moon was not to be found beyond the mountains, but now she was more curious than ever.

Dark clouds covered the Sun and rain began to fall, as the sky battled with a storm.

As night-time fell, the Moon peeped out from
behind the raging black clouds. Luna tried
as hard as she could to stay awake.
Drip, drop, splished the rain,
drippy
drop...

drip

drop

drip

drop

Soon, Luna's eyes were closing and she was
drifting into a dreamy sleep, pondering if perhaps
the Moon might hide behind the clouds all day...

Luna's dream took her way up high, above the clouds.

There, bright and beaming, she found the Sun, just as dazzling as the Moon... but no sign of the Moon at all.

The storm had passed by morning, and Luna could see the Sun,
trying to shine through the watery clouds.
But where on earth was the Moon?
Luna had pondered and puzzled, looked and listened.
Perhaps she would never, ever walk on the Moon,
surrounded by twinkling stars.

That evening, Luna walked glumly from the window and climbed into bed.
As her eyes closed and she drifted into a dreamy sleep,
the Moon seemed further away than ever.

Could there be a place Luna hadn't searched — beyond the ocean, higher than
the mountains, further than the clouds — where the Moon might live?

Luna's dream took her far, far away — into space. There, dancing in the darkness, she found the Moon at long last. It was brighter than the stars and round as a button, as beautiful as it was on the night she was born.

"Hurry home, Luna," whispered the Moon softly, "it's bedtime."
"But where do you go in the daytime?" Luna asked, and the Moon replied,
"I'm always here in space, watching over you. You just can't see me in the daytime."

That night, and forever after, Luna slept peacefully, knowing that the Moon lived in space and appeared in the sky to check on her when night-time fell.

But, being a curious little girl, Luna soon began to ask herself...

"where on earth is space?"

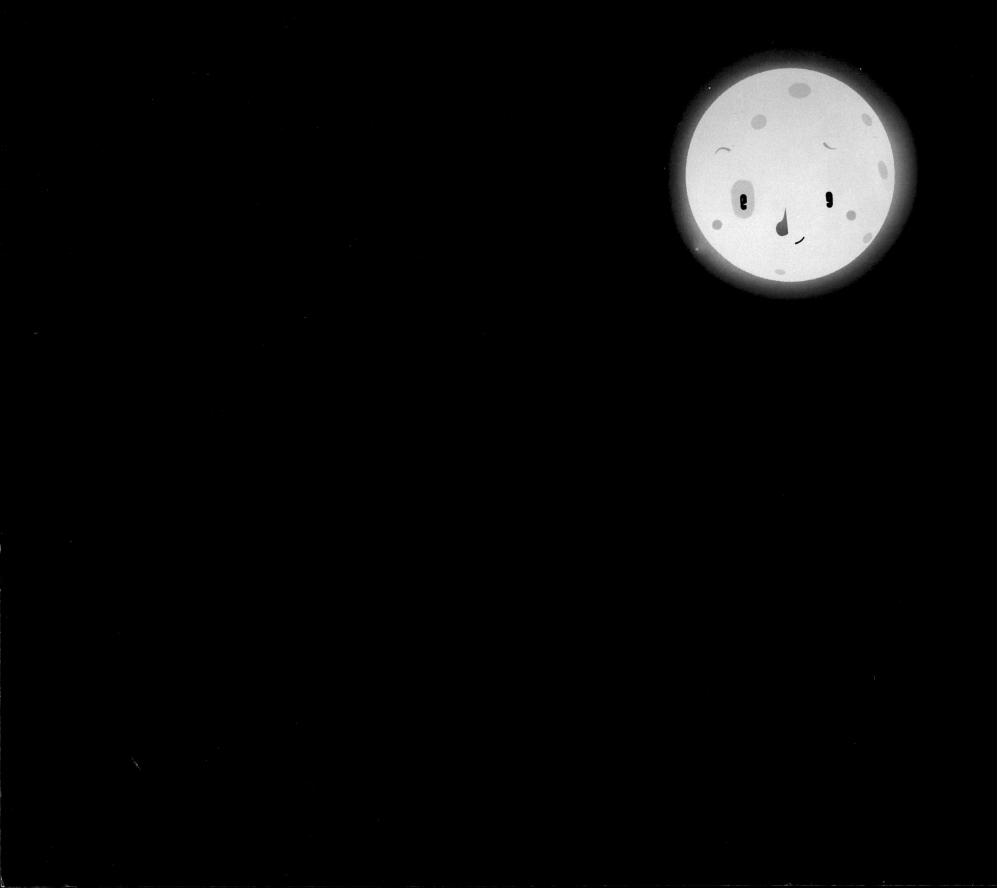